Boggarts
of
Britain

FRANK MILLS

Boggarts of Britain

Oldcastle Books

This edition published in 2000 by Oldcastle Books,
18 Coleswood Road, Harpenden, Herts, AL5 1EQ

Copyright © Frank Mills 2000

The right of Frank Mills to be identified as author of
this work has been asserted by him in accordance with
the Copyright, Designs & Patents Act 1988.

All rights reserved. No part of this book may be
reproduced, stored in or introduced into a retrieval
system, or transmitted, in any form or by any means
(electronic, mechanical, photocopying, recording or
otherwise) without the written permission of the
publishers. Any person who does any unauthorised act
in relation to this publication may be liable to criminal
prosecution and civil claims for damages.

A CIP catalogue record for this book is available

ISBN 1-84243-005-X Boggarts of Britain

2 4 6 8 10 9 7 5 3 1

Typeset by Koinonia, Manchester
Printed by Omnia

For Sinericon

ACKNOWLEDGEMENTS

I am grateful to the children of Cheddar First School for their encouraging appraisal of these stories.

CONTENTS

Boggart Hole Clough   13

Boggart Farm   37

Boggart Rescue   57

Boggarts Underground   91

AUTHOR'S NOTE

Stories have been told about a race of little people called Boggarts for at least a hundred and fifty years.

They are always dressed in brown with little smudges of green and some reports say they can be as small as fifty centimetres high while others say they are more than twice as tall.

Because Boggarts are so small, people think they are weak but this is not so. Inside their small bodies there is a tremendous amount of special energy which allows them to perform tasks with such speed and accuracy that it has all the appearance of magic.

They are not spiteful or dangerous and they never mean to hurt anyone deliberately; but they do have a great sense of fun which, sometimes, leads them into serious mischief and it is at these times that some people say they dislike them.

However, all the reports say that Boggarts are always bright and cheerful and that they love singing and dancing.

BOGGART HOLE CLOUGH

A long time ago in the County of Lancashire there was a place called Boggart Hole Clough. It might still be there for all I know because the people who live in the nearby village do say that if you look carefully three nights after the moon rises, at about twelve o'clock midnight, you can still see traces of blackened woodwork and sometimes even a few wisps of smoke rising from the ground.

If you happened to be passing at that time of night I expect you would be just a little worried, so perhaps you would like to know how it got its name and how these strange things came about.

It must be a hundred years since Thomas Fraser built his house on this very spot. He did not believe all the stories the villagers told him about it being the home of the Pixies and to tell the truth he was not very interested.

"Pixies!" he said. "Pah! Who believes in Pixies nowadays?"

When they told him that it was not always Pixies who cast their spell over the land but Fairies as well and even Boggarts, he burst out laughing in their faces.

"Boggarts!" he spluttered. "You'll be telling me next there are ghosts and things that go bump in the night."

Mr. Fraser had heard stories like this before. Where he used to live some people believed in ghosts so much that when they said their prayers at night they would often put in a special piece at the end:

*From ghoulies and ghaisties
and lang-leggit beasties
and things that go bump in the night
Good Lord deliver us.*

So Mr. Fraser laughed at the Pixies and the Boggarts and built his house. He built it partly of brick and partly of wood and he made it firm and safe against the winds and the rains and the snow and the thunder and the lightning. From all these he made it safe.

"Ay," said the folk in the village, "he's made it safe enough from the weather. But has he made it safe from Boggarts?"

"Boggarts be blowed!" scoffed Mr. Fraser. "There are no such things and if you want to go on believing there are, you're welcome but don't come fussing round my door with your silly tales."

"You'll find they're not silly before you've been in the place a week," they warned him.

"Maybe I shall; and maybe I shan't," said Mr. Fraser, "but I'll tell you what I'll do. I'll dig a big hole at the bottom of my garden and the Boggarts can live in there. All of them. That shows you how much I care about them."

He did just that. He dug a hole and he invited all his neighbours to send their Boggarts to live in his hole. The villagers went away shaking their heads and muttering to themselves but the strange thing is that although nobody ever remembers seeing a Boggart to tell them about

Mr. Fraser's invitation, somehow or other ... they got to know!

Now a Boggart is a very special kind of Imp. He loves mischief and playing jokes on people. He is never really wicked in his tricks but of all the little people in the world that Mr. Fraser could choose to live at the bottom of his garden, the Boggarts are just about the worst. He began to wonder about them the day he moved in and after three days he was convinced. His wife was quite sure long before that and, for the sake of the children, she tried to persuade him to make friends with them and perhaps to say publicly that he did really believe in them. Mr. Fraser snorted.

"If you think I'm going to stand out there in the middle of the moor and tell nobody in particular that I believe in Pixies or Boggarts, or whatever you call them, you are very much mistaken. This is my house and I'll live in it. I'll invite whoever I want to see and I'll make my own friends. Is that clear?"

It was very clear. It was clear to Mrs. Fraser; and it was also clear to the children. It was clear to the neighbours and ... it was also clear to the Boggarts. On the night of the new moon, Mr. Fraser moved in to his house that was safe from the weather and, to show that he was not impressed by the neighbours' silly gossip, he made a notice board and put it beside the hole he had dug at the bottom of his garden. On the board he wrote:

BOGGART HOLE

Then he went indoors to bed. To bed; but not to sleep. In ten minutes his son, Richard, came running into his bedroom calling out that his bed was going up and down and he could not get to sleep.

"Nonsense," said Mr. Fraser. "You've been listening to rubbish. Go back to bed."

In vain the boy insisted that he was not making it up. His father was not going to be persuaded into believing the silly stories.

"You have been listening to the neighbours," he snapped. "Go back to bed this instant and let's have no more tomfoolery."

Slowly, the boy went back to bed and for half an hour everything was quiet. Mr. Fraser lay in his bed, congratulating himself on his fine house and laughed quietly to himself when he thought of all the silly tales that country folk believe in. He sighed contentedly and turned over to go to sleep when the door burst open with a crash and his daughter, Molly, came in crying out that all the bedclothes had been pulled off her as she slept and that the bed was going up and down like a see-saw. Mr. Fraser was now really annoyed. He was annoyed at being disturbed for a second time and he was annoyed at the neighbours for frightening the children with their silly legends. He jumped out of bed and marched down the passage to where Molly had been sleeping.

"I'll soon settle this," he grunted; and strode on. Inside the room he stopped for a moment to look at the scene. Bedclothes were all over the floor, the bed itself had been pushed away from the wall and...was it his imagination or did he see the mattress gradually sink in the middle? He picked up the bedclothes and made the bed again.

He looked out of the window to see if he could catch any sign of creeping villagers because he still thought they were responsible for all these tricks. But the night was quite still. At the bottom of the garden he could make out the vague outline of the notice board he had put up but there was no movement around it. He comforted Molly, said goodnight and popped her back into bed. Molly was not very keen on staying there on her own but she was going to try very hard to settle down to sleep. Mr. Fraser returned to his room.

"I told you no good would come of this," said his wife miserably.

"Oh, don't talk such rubbish. They may have believed in Boggarts two hundred years ago; but I tell you once and for all there are no such things as Boggarts to-day."

Perhaps he should have spoken a little more softly because just as he finished speaking there was a tremendous crash outside the front door and his wife began to shiver with fright.

"What was that?" she whispered, between chattering teeth.

"Wind!" said Mr. Fraser, a little uneasily and stretched himself out in the bed.

The next instant he was sitting bolt upright while Mrs. Fraser had disappeared under the bedclothes. Without any doubt at all this time, someone was knocking on the front door.

"Don't answer it, don't answer it," pleaded his wife in muffled tones from somewhere inside the bed, but Mr. Fraser climbed out of bed for the third time.

"Don't be foolish. Who do you think it is?"

"Boggarts!" replied his wife, simply.

"Nonsense. If it were Boggarts they wouldn't wait to knock on the door, would they? They would just walk in."

"Ah, so you do believe in them."

"I didn't say anything of the sort; but if they can do the things you say they can do, I should think they could manage a little thing like a front door."

He went downstairs and pulled back the bolts on the front door. Slowly the door opened and he looked out. Not six feet from where he stood shivering in the night breeze, facing him and stuck firmly in the ground, was the notice board with the words staring him in the face:

BOGGART HOLE

Somebody had moved the board. He shut the door quickly, pushed home all the bolts and, with a quick look all around him, went smartly upstairs to bed, a lot more worried than he was prepared to admit to anyone.

"One of those silly villagers," he growled, "playing tricks and stupid games; moving the notice board I put up this morning. I'll give them a piece of my mind when I get up."

"Moved the board, did you say?"

"Yes—stuck it outside the door. They're like a lot of mischievous children."

"Supposing it wasn't the villagers?"

"Oh, don't start that all over again. I'm fed up with the word Boggart and I'd be obliged if you don't mention it again."

Richard and Molly gritted their teeth. They were determined not to give in to the bumps and noises they heard in the night and eventually they became so tired that even the revels and midnight games going on all round the house and garden could not keep them awake and they went to sleep.

The next morning, before Thomas Fraser could go out and tell the villagers what he thought of them for playing silly pranks in the night, the villagers came to him. They thanked him for the most comfortable night they had enjoyed for years.

"Seems they heard all about your invitation, Mr. Fraser. They've all gone to live in your Boggart Hole."

"I hope they stay there," said another one. "It's quite a treat not to hear bumps and slithers all through the night."

They sympathised with him when he told them about the board but they all thought he deserved it for the way he had gone on about the Boggarts.

"I'll never believe in Boggarts, I tell you. You're all living in ancient times up here. Nobody believes in things like that any more, except the children."

"Ay, that shows their good sense," said one of the neighbours.

"They'll never leave you alone

now," said another one, "not until you do what we all do and leave a bowl of cream on the doorstep for them to eat in the night."

"Do you mean you leave perfectly good cream outside the door every night, before you go to bed?"

"Of course we do. If we didn't we would always have a night like you had by the sound of things."

"But there are no such things as Boggarts!"

"Well, who eats the cream then?"

"Do you mean it's gone in the morning?"

"The bowls are still there but the cream has gone."

"Then all I can say is that the cats and dogs round here must be having the time of their lives."

"You take our advice," they told him, "put some cream out."

"I'll give them cream," grunted Mr. Fraser. "I'll give 'em cream."

During the day he put the notice board back where it belonged and he worked on it rather longer than you would expect.

When night began to fall he inspected his work and it could be seen that he had driven in nails all over the post so that they would stick out on the other side. Anybody who tried to move the board now would be very lucky not to catch their hands on the nails.

They did not move the post. In fact nothing was heard all through the night although that did not help Mr. Fraser much because he was awake most of the night listening for them, ready to rush downstairs to catch them in the act.

But nothing happened in the night. Next morning almost everything did. Just as Mr. Fraser was getting up the bedclothes began to move and, before he knew what was happening, the sheets were being shaken with him still inside them. Then they were thrown into the corner of the room and it was nearly five minutes before he could disentangle himself from all the folds. When he did get free, he tried to go downstairs but could not open the door. Shaking with rage, he put his foot against the wall and put all his strength into pulling at the handle. Unfortunately for him the door was released at just that moment and Mr. Fraser found himself on the floor once again, this time with the door on top of him. Tenderly, he felt his nose to see if it was broken before he walked through the space where the door had been.

When he arrived at the top of the stairs, the mat slipped and he bumped his way down to the bottom getting quicker and quicker as he went; and when he sat down to breakfast he leapt up in the air as quick as lightning. There on his seat were the nails he had driven into the notice board the day before.

The children could not stop laughing, which only made his temper worse, but Molly's laughter did stop when her bowl suddenly turned upside down and her porridge landed in her lap. Richard was laughing so much that his orange juice dribbled down his chin and down inside his shirt, while Mrs. Fraser found that the butter had melted and was running all over the tablecloth.

Breakfast was abandoned with Mrs. Fraser appealing once again for Mr. Fraser to put out some cream as the villagers suggested and to say loudly that he did not mean it when he said there were no Boggarts any more. But Mr. Fraser was stubborn.

"I'll not apologise to something I can't even see and I'll certainly not waste good food on every stray cat and dog in the neighbourhood. I won't. I won't. I'll set fire to the place first before I give in."

Somehow the day passed. Mr. and Mrs. Fraser became more and more irritable because they had not slept for two nights. The children were frightening themselves by listening to stories in the village and then making up worse ones of their own— and night approached—the second night after the rising of the new moon.

During the afternoon, Mr. Fraser went into the big town and when he came back he carried a shotgun in his arms. He rode slowly through the village showing everybody the gun.

"Anybody who comes near my house to-night will wish he hadn't," he said grimly.

Nobody wanted to go near his house. If they were offered payment to go near the house nobody would accept it. All the same, things happened. As soon as darkness fell, the windows began to rattle and Mr. Fraser went outside with his shotgun but there was nobody around.

What is more, there was no trace of any wind; yet the windows continued to rattle. He sent his family to bed with strict instructions to stay there whatever happened. He then prowled round the house with his shotgun, rousing himself to a greater and greater pitch of temper as every minute passed. The doors began to shake, clothes slid off hangers, windows burst open and great gusts of wind whistled through the rooms. Outside, there was not so much as a gentle breeze.

Suddenly the front door banged and Mr. Fraser raced downstairs with his gun ready to fire. Nobody in sight. With a swish, the lights in the hall went out and the door slammed. Mr. Fraser rushed to it just as it opened again and, for the second time that day, he tenderly nursed his flattened nose. The door was still open and he noticed a vague shape outside. He raised his gun to his shoulder but the shape disappeared and he raced out into the night in hot pursuit. The door behind him slammed shut. He was locked out.

He called to his wife, to Richard, to Molly telling them to come and let him in but they had been told to stay where they were—whatever happened. For nearly an hour he wandered morosely around the garden but although he did not believe in them, he took good care not to go near the Boggart Hole.

After an hour he could stand it no longer. He threw a brick through the window and climbed back into his newly built house. When he went upstairs he found a terrified wife who thought he was a Boggart walking up the stairs.

"A very big Boggart," grunted Mr. Fraser.

"I'll not stay another night in this house," sobbed Mrs. Fraser.

"All right, all right," agreed her husband. "We'll move tomorrow. But I won't be beaten. I won't be beaten by a gang of imps playing mischievous pranks. I'll finish those Boggarts—or whatever they are—or my name is not Thomas Fraser."

At last the dawn came to a very weary and red-eyed family. Mr. Fraser took his wife and family to the town and booked them into an inn. Then he came back and loaded most of his belongings on to his cart and drove slowly back to the inn. When he brought the cart back again he had several large cans which he unloaded. He loaded the empty cart with all of his remaining goods and set to work on the house.

He soaked the whole house with paraffin from the cans and did his work so thoroughly that it was nearly dark by the time he had finished. He turned the horse and cart so that it was facing the way to the inn.

For the last time he looked around his new house; the house he had moved into only three days before. Then solemnly and stubbornly he set fire to his own property and stood back as the flames blazed through the rooms, upstairs and downstairs; up to the roof and out to the garden. In the light from the fire he saw the words "Boggart Hole" and chuckled to himself.

As the flames finally died down the moon shone brightly on the blackened timbers and the thin wisps of smoke still swirling upwards.

It was the third night after the new moon. He climbed into the cart and shook the reins.

"At last," he sighed, "that's got rid of you," and he drove off into the night. Just by his side, one of the milk churns began to twist and grind with a whirring noise. He turned his head to stare with sudden alarm as the cap twisted right off and out popped a little figure dressed in green and brown. He sat on the top of the churn and crossed his tiny legs in a most carefree manner. He was smiling all over his jolly little face and he began to hum a little tune. He nodded brightly to Mr. Fraser.

"Quick work, that," he chirruped. "We only just got out of there in time."

Before Mr. Fraser's astonished gaze, the little man began to whistle.

Mr. Fraser's own personal Boggart had definitely come to stay.

BOGGART FARM

Out in the open countryside, not very far from the city of Denbury, there is a fine big farm with new sheds and new barns and a large red brick farmhouse beautifully furnished with all the most modern and most comfortable furniture. If you were to look a little more carefully you would see that just at the back of the farmhouse, looking very out of place amongst all the new buildings, there is a very old, ramshackle barn that looks as though it would fall over in a strong wind.

The owner of the farm is Mr. Philip Spencer and the field where the farmhouse and the old barn stand has been in Mr. Spencer's family for over one hundred and fifty years.

Many times people have asked him why he doesn't knock the old barn down and build a new one to match the other modern ones but Mr. Spencer just shakes his head and says:

"I know why I don't and there's others who know why." That is all he would say.

Inside the farmhouse the kitchen is large and airy with electric machines of all kinds which makes it all the more surprising to find, hanging behind the door, a bundle! A bundle of rags! A bundle of rags that seems very much out of place amongst all this tidiness. At first it looks as if it is all brown in colour but when you get close you can see faint smudges of green as well. Nobody ever touches it and how it stays in one piece is a little bit of a mystery in itself. It is never brushed but no dust ever settles on it. It has never been repaired but it never becomes more ragged.

In fact, Mr. Spencer will tell you that it is exactly the same as it was when he was a boy, when it hung in exactly the same place as it hangs today.

But it was not Mr. Spencer's father who had put it there nor even his father's father. It was the very first Mr. Spencer—the one who had bought the farm with its one cottage, one barn and one field—over one hundred and fifty years ago.

He had put it there and had told

his children that it must never be moved and that they should tell their children that it must never be moved.

So the present Mr. Spencer's father had told him and Mr. Spencer had kept it just as it was all those years ago.

The farm has grown in size, the land has been cleared to make room for more buildings and the present Mr. Spencer has bought harvesters and tractors and ploughs and of course he has built his fine new farmhouse.

Behind the fine new farmhouse stands—or leans—or wobbles—the old barn! He would never dream of knocking it down just as he would never dream of touching the bundle of green and brown rags that hangs behind the kitchen door.

Why should it be so special?

When the first Mr. Spencer, whose name was George, had bought the farm it was a great struggle to grow enough to feed his family. If the summer was bad or the winter was very hard they would be hungry for many days, even weeks, and there were times when he was tempted to give up the farm altogether. The work was too hard for one man and although Mrs. Spencer helped as much as she could she had two small children who needed a lot of her time. But every time they thought of giving up they reminded themselves of what they had. They had their cottage and they had their field and they had their barn.

One year the winter had been very hard and the summer that followed was very wet. It seemed as though, this year, the better times were not coming at all and George, as he looked around his small field and gazed at the sky, sighed when he realised that the summer was almost over and next winter would soon be upon them. There was practically nothing to show for the summer's work; and very little in the barn to see them through the winter.

He made up his mind that he would ride to Denbury the very next day to see if anybody would buy his farm. By selling up, he might have enough to start all over again—perhaps in another part of the country where he might have better luck.

But the people in Denbury knew all about the farm. They had told him that it was too much for one man and how foolish he had been to risk all his money in such a way. They were sorry for him but, sadly, nobody would buy his one field and his barn and his cottage.

He returned home and sat glumly in the kitchen. The barn was silent. There was no threshing to be done. At last Mrs. Spencer persuaded him to go to bed but although he agreed it was of little use. He lay awake all through the night thinking of plans to save the farm and make it pay enough to keep his family.

At last he began to nod sleepily and finally he slipped off into sleep.

Suddenly he sat bolt upright in bed. There was a noise; he was quite sure he heard a noise. Was it downstairs or was it outside? He slipped out of bed and into his clothes and crept quietly downstairs. As he passed the window that looked out on the back of the house he heard the noise again. There was no mistake this time. He looked out into the grey night. There it was again. He was right. It came from the old barn!

Carefully and very quietly, he tiptoed across to the barn and gently lifted the latch on the door. Then with a quick swing he flung open the door. Empty! The barn was empty—

or was it? Determined to make sure, he slithered along the wall to where he knew the lantern was hanging and when it was alight he held it high above his head. There was nobody in the barn, nobody at all. He turned back towards the door and stopped in his tracks with a gasp of surprise. All along one wall, reaching half way to the roof, newly threshed corn was stacked, corn he knew was not there in the afternoon.

For some minutes he did nothing but stare at the sight and then, with a shout, he raced across to the house where he roused his wife, pouring out the story of what he had seen and asking if she knew what it all meant. Mrs. Spencer knew nothing about it. To tell the truth she did not even know what her husband was talking about and she set about the difficult task of getting him to calm down.

They finally decided to wait for

morning when the dark could no longer play tricks on them, because Mrs. Spencer was beginning to worry that her husband had been overcome by the trouble they were in and was seeing things that were not there and hearing things which nobody else had heard.

In the morning they opened the barn door very carefully with Mr. Spencer fearing that he had imagined it all and that they would find the barn empty, as it had been twenty four hours earlier. He allowed his wife to go in first and as soon as he heard the sudden gasp he pushed past her and looked along the wall. He had not imagined anything. The wall was just as he had seen it, half full of corn.

They searched the barn from top to bottom for some sign to tell them how it had happened. But although they searched in every corner until they were worn out, no clue could they find.

Mr. Spencer stayed up late that night hoping to hear the noise again but he was so tired with all the searching that, just after midnight, he fell fast asleep in the big armchair by the fire.

That was exactly where his wife found him in the morning when she came to tell him that corn was now stacked along another wall and, what was more, the kitchen had been scrubbed and cleaned and everything had been left ready for breakfast. George said not a word but walked deliberately across to the old barn and opened the door. For some minutes he stood gazing at the sight and then walked slowly back to the house, shaking his head in bewilderment.

The following morning the work had been done again and the barn was half full of fine rich corn, much better than any crop Mr. Spencer had seen before. He told his wife he was thinking of selling it before the dream disappeared leaving the old barn empty again, but she persuaded him to wait for one more night and find a hiding place in the barn so that they might discover how it all happened. He wasn't too sure about this, partly because he was afraid that if they were watching it would stop and partly because he was the tiniest little bit...just afraid!

Finally he agreed and just before midnight they hid themselves in the barn and waited. Mrs. Spencer began to doze off and then woke with a start because George was already snoring. She kept pushing him to keep him awake and after about the twentieth time she suddenly clutched his arm, pinching it with such force that he only just stopped himself from crying out.

There, in the middle of the barn, stood the tiniest little man they had ever seen. He looked no more than fifty centimetres high and was dressed in a little suit of brown and green. He sang little snatches of cheerful songs as he wielded a flail at a tremendous rate while corn that George had never seen before lay stacked in every corner of the barn. What a sight George and his wife must have looked, half sitting and half kneeling, their mouths wide open in amazement, Mrs. Spencer with her hand clutching George's arm and he too surprised to remember that she was hurting him.

By the time morning came they were hemmed in by corn and they had to fight their way out. For a long time George said nothing because he was afraid that his wife had not seen what he had seen and would think he was making it up. Eventually he could not keep it to himself any longer and blurted out all the details of the astonishing sight. To his great relief, his wife said she had seen exactly the same and by the time they were ready to go to bed they had decided on a plan. This time they would watch the kitchen because there was no more room for the tiny man to work in the barn. During the night they crept downstairs and gently pushed open the door just enough to be able to peep inside. Their eyes nearly popped out of their heads at the sight that met them!

Half a dozen tiny people, no bigger than their friend from the barn, were hopping and prancing around the kitchen singing and whistling as cheerfully as anything while they attended to all the work which Mrs. Spencer found done every morning. Whether they were sweeping the dust or laying the table they were all whistling or singing the very same song.

Snoring and sleeping,
the kitchen needs sweeping,
The dishes are under our feet.
Now the floor has been rubbered,
The cat's in the cupboard
And everything's tidy and neat.

Quietly George and his wife crept back to bed.

The very next day George went into Denbury to arrange to sell his corn. He went to all the people who had refused to buy his farm; and he went to all the people who had told him the work was too much for one man; and he invited them all to come and see what he had to sell. Cheerfully, he galloped back to the farm in the late afternoon, with the red sun dropping down behind him as he rode and with a sharp evening breeze beginning to blow. What could he give to the little man who had changed his whole life for him? How could he show that he was grateful to him and all his tiny friends? He thought of how he had stood in the middle of the barn flashing that flail faster than anything he had ever seen and that little, ragged brown suit! He jumped off his horse as he reached the farmhouse and called out to his wife.

Of course that was it. The little man needed a new suit. It was so tiny his wife could make it in no time at all ... and she did. It was finished in good time and just before they went to bed they crept out to the barn and laid the tiny suit on the floor. They smiled as they saw how small it was and yet how strong was the spell of the person who would wear it. Happier than they had been for many months, they returned to the house.

But they could not sleep. George kept dozing and dreaming that all his fine corn had been burnt in a fire. Mrs. Spencer was awake wondering if the suit would fit. At one o'clock they could stand it no longer. They crept downstairs, past the kitchen which was absolutely quiet and then on out of the house. All the ground between the house and the barn was lit by moonlight and for a moment they thought of going back. But curiosity overcame them and they slipped softly from patch to patch until they arrived at the door of the barn. Mrs. Spencer pulled at George's sleeve to show that she had found a little crack in the boards and, together, they peeped through. They were only just in time.

The little man was there and was wearing the new suit. It fitted perfectly.

The corn was still there, safe and sound, but the little man did not look as happy as usual. He was not doing any work and he was not smiling.

He just walked up and down and rubbed the sleeve of his new suit.

They began to worry that they had done the wrong thing and the very next minute they were sure. The little man began to dance but slowly and sadly and when he started to sing, it was just as quietly and a little mournfully:

*Boggart fine and Boggart spry
Boggart now away will fly.*

In a flash he was gone!

They craned their necks to see into all the corners of the old barn.

They opened the door and searched first by the light of the moon and then by the newly lit lantern. The little man had gone and all that was left, apart from the corn, was a little ragged suit of brown and green.

Sadly, they went back to the house and looked in the kitchen. Empty. No sound. The little men had all gone but as they turned away they heard a voice singing, slowly but very distinctly:

Because you gave us himpen hampen
We will no more bolt nor stampen.
'Tis not your garments, new or old,
That Boggarts need—they feel no cold.
If milk or cream you leave each day
Good fortune at our farm will stay.
But as you left no drop or crumb
Boggarts never more will come.

So George Spencer knew that his little friends would never come again.

But they had given him the chance to make his farm a success and he took the chance.

He hung the little ragged suit

behind the kitchen door and told his wife and his children that there the bundle would stay. They must tell their children not to disturb it or the prosperity of the farm would melt away. All the children of the Spencer family have passed on the message and that is why you will find a little bundle of rags behind the door, which is never touched, never dusted, never disturbed, never mended … and never grows any older. There is one other duty passed down to all the children of the Spencer family. They have a task to set a bowl of fresh cream on the kitchen table every evening and there it stays all night. It is a duty that must be carried out because of what George and his wife heard on that night when all the little people flew away. It is set for a little man they know will never come.

BOGGART RESCUE

Many, many years ago, on the coast of Britain, stood a great castle called the Castle of Zoclan. This was the home of a great warrior, a stern but very just man, known to his people as the Duke of Zo.

On this day, the castle is full of activity, with soldiers and serving men riding in and out, taking messages or bringing in supplies while the fine horses are being groomed and prepared for a very long journey.

Inside the castle, in the great Council Chamber itself, noblemen are listening intently to the Duke explaining why he has brought them here.

"My cousin, the Prince, has asked for my help against a strong army of rebels who have laid waste to his land and threatened his people.

They have conquered large parts of the Province and are rapidly approaching his Palace. He cannot hold out for very long and I intend to ride to his support."

The noblemen began to talk about the Duke's plan and he could see that many of them were nodding their heads in agreement. But he was growing impatient at the time they were taking and, as he strode to the window to point out how peaceful were the long, rolling fields of their land, his great size made the floor shake.

"Come with me," he called in ringing tones, "we'll send these rebels packing and be back in our own castles before six months have passed."

They hesitated no longer. With a loud cheer, they pledged their soldiers to fight to free the Prince's land from the invaders and they knew that, with a strong leader like the Duke of Zo, they could defeat any enemy.

Before many days had passed they were almost ready to go. Messages came pouring into Zoclan Castle to say that from far and wide the nobles were coming with their armies to join the mighty Duke of Zo.

From Zoclan Castle they would start their journey to the Prince's land, many miles away. Outside, excitement was growing. The horses were stamping their feet, impatient to be away; soldiers were drawn up ready to march; grooms were rushing about making last minute alterations, repairing straps, replacing faulty weapons and giving a last pat to the horses they had looked after for so many weeks. The time for preparation was over. The time for action had come.

Twenty yards from the huge gates of the castle trudged a very small boy dressed in ragged clothes and carrying a tiny can. He had walked for many miles that hot summer morning and he looked as though he was about to fall to the ground with weariness. Yet he managed to stagger to the gates of the castle and weakly knocked with little hands against the massive iron bars. Nobody answered. For who should hear such a tiny tap in the midst of the noise and preparation for departure? Nobody heard.

Just then, a soldier came riding from the gate. Steam was already rising from his horse's flanks, for it was not many minutes since he had been the bearer of tidings telling of another great noble, who had left his castle and was marching to meet the Duke in a valley two miles north of the castle of Zoclan.

Just for a second or two the gates swung open as the rider spurred through and, in that brief moment, the little boy slipped quietly into the courtyard.

In the bustle and excitement he passed unnoticed. He gazed with wonder at the dazzling colour of the soldiers' uniforms and saw the fine sheen on the horses' flanks. Flags and banners fluttered slowly in the small breeze as the grooms, their work done, retired to the sides of the courtyard, leaving the centre free for the nobles and for the Duke himself.

One of the stewards, backing away from the scene of all this excitement, nearly tripped over the ragged little boy as he stood there, his tiny can still clasped in his hand, his face dirty and scratched with little smears of blood, his clothes torn and almost falling from his back, his eyes bright with interest at the fine sight in front of him.

This steward was a disagreeable man and did not like being pushed into the background by the soldiers. He was even envious of the Duke himself. He did not like dirty little boys; and especially he did not like them when they crept into places where they did not belong.

"What are you doing here?" he called, gruffly.

The boy started back at the sound of the harsh voice so close to him and he tried to disappear into the shadows of the wall, but the steward held him fast.

"Do you hear me, boy? What are you doing? Spying?"

The boy shook his head as hard as he could and tried again to escape from the clutches of the man. He grasped his can still tighter in case he should lose it and the steward noticed the action.

"Ha! What have you there?"

The boy licked his lips and tried to speak but the words would not come.

"Been stealing, have you? Well, I know how to deal with people who steal."

At this, the boy managed to find his voice. His tongue was very dry but he pushed it between his lips until, slowly and with great difficulty, the sounds came out.

"Please sir, I haven't stolen anything. This is my can. I brought it for some wine."

"For some what?" thundered the

steward so loudly that many of the other stewards and some of the soldiers stared in his direction. None of them liked this particular steward because they all knew how he enjoyed bullying people who could not answer back. They smiled and admired the way the little boy spoke up for himself.

"Please sir, for some wine. My mother is very ill but this wine will make her well again."

"That's a fine story. I've heard that sort of yarn before. Off with you. Go on, sharp now; or I'll take the whip to you."

The boy was not listening. His gaze was fixed on the centre of the courtyard where, standing half a head above all the others, his dazzling armour glistening in the rays of the sun, his bright plumes shining like the first rainbow after a storm, stood the Duke of Zo himself.

Beside him stood the most magnificent horse the boy had ever seen, the brilliant harnesses reflecting back the sun like golden mirrors. So determined was the boy's gaze and so steadfast his eyes that, after a minute or two, the Duke began to look about him as though something was directing him to turn. Gradually his eyes came round to the ragged urchin standing in the grasp of one of his stewards and, without a moment's hesitation, he strode across to where they stood.

"Why are you holding the boy?" he asked, curtly.

"I found him creeping along the wall, your Grace, and when I caught him I saw that he had been stealing."

"Stealing what?"

"This can, sir. Look how greedily he clutches it to himself."

"Show me the can," said the Duke and held out his hand for it.

The boy clenched his fingers on the tiny can and looked up at the great figure before him.

"Please, sir, I may not. None but I may hold it."

"Insolent boy," snapped the steward. "Don't you know who you are talking to?"

"Don't interrupt me," said the Duke, sharply. "You will speak when I ask you to speak."

The steward cringed away, conscious that everybody who was watching was pleased to hear the Duke talk to him so sharply. The Duke turned back to the boy.

"Now, boy," he said quietly. "Do you know who I am?"

"Yes sir," replied the boy. "You are the Duke of Zo."

"And still you will not show me?"

"My mother says I may not let it from my hand."

"You are a very obedient boy.

Suppose I take it from you. What will you do then?"

"You will not try, sir. I know you will not try."

"How do you know?"

"Because I know that you are stern but you are just. You will not ask me to give up something which is mine."

"Well spoken. I will not indeed. Tell me the truth, boy. Did you steal the can?"

"No, sir. I did not. It was my mother's can and she gave it to me this morning to bring here to the castle."

"Why?"

"I was told to have it filled with wine."

"That little can will hold very little wine. For what purpose do you want the wine?"

"My mother is very ill, sir. There is a story which has been passed down in our family that if the oldest becomes ill, then the youngest, however small, must take this can to the castle of Zoclan and have it filled with wine. If he fails, the oldest one will die; but if he succeeds, the oldest will be made well again. I have walked ten miles to fill the can."

By this time, all the other nobles had gathered round the Duke and when they heard this last remark they burst out laughing and made jokes about the ragged boy. But the Duke turned to look at them and, at the sight of his face, they stopped laughing. He turned back to the steward.

"Let the boy go," he commanded, "and go back to your sweeping which is all you will ever be fit for."

The surly look which came over the steward's face boded ill for the Duke but by that time he had turned to another of his men, a trusted follower who had served him well for many years.

"Take the boy to the castle. Give him food and find some clothes for him; if we have anything that small. Then take him to the wine cellar and fill his can with the best wine. Then see that he returns safely to his mother. If he tries to walk another ten miles, neither he nor the wine will get home."

"I do not ask for the best wine, sir. Only that my can shall be filled."

"That should not take very long. Very well; you may use any wine in the cellar except that cask which is marked with a red square. That is the last cask prepared by my ancestors long ago and it is the finest in my land. Like you, my boy, things are passed down in my family too; and give my best regards to your mother."

The Duke turned away to organize the final preparations for departure. The soldier nodded to the boy and led him into the castle and down some steps. They reached a thick wooden door which the man opened with a key and then down more steps into the cellar of the Castle of Zoclan.

The boy had never seen such a sight before. The cellar was full of huge casks of wine and the man led him to a cask which was half full.

He held out his hand for the can but the boy repeated what he had told the Duke and held the can himself while the man poured the wine.

After a few minutes a look of amazement spread across the soldier's face and quickly he looked at the cask of wine. Slowly he tipped it up until the last trickle had finished and then, unbelievingly, he looked at the tiny can still held firmly in the boy's hand. It was less than a quarter full.

"You're not as simple as you look. This can is bigger than I thought."

"Much bigger," agreed the boy.

"There's some trickery here," grumbled the soldier. "I have poured half a cask full of wine into that little can and it is not nearly full. I'll not open another cask for a simple job like this."

"The Duke told you to fill the can," argued the boy. "Are you going to disobey his instructions?"

"I've poured out enough wine to fill this little can a dozen times over."

"But you haven't filled it."

"No; and I'll not fill it if it means opening a new cask. The Duke will be away by now, so you had better take what you have and go."

But the Duke had not gone. He had come into the castle to make sure his instructions had been obeyed and he stood now at the top of the cellar steps.

"Come, have you not carried out this simple task? It's a small enough can you have been asked to fill."

The soldier was startled by the sound of the Duke's voice and he was only able to mumble as he tried to answer.

"It seems small enough," he agreed, "but I have emptied half a cask already and the can is less than a quarter full."

"Then it must have a hole in the bottom. Look for it!"

But although the soldier looked and the Duke came down himself to look, they could find no hole. What is more, they could not find a single drop of wine spilled on the floor. It was as clean as it had been when they started pouring.

"It's witchcraft, that's what it is," muttered the soldier. "I want nothing to do with it."

"You must carry out the task you were set," commanded the Duke, without raising his voice, because he could see the man who had served him so well was becoming more and more upset.

"Now," he said, turning to the little urchin who was still holding the tiny can. "What can you tell us about this strange business?"

"You said you would fill my can, sir but it is less than a quarter full."

Many of the other serving men had gathered at the top of the stairs when they heard the ragged boy answering the Duke of Zo in so calm a manner. Some of the nobles, impatient to be off, had also come into the castle to find out what was keeping the Duke and they pushed the men out of the way to see what was going on.

They expected to see a very angry Duke indeed, but they were wrong. The Duke was not angry at all. He was curious to know what was so special about this tiny boy who spoke with such assurance and he was looking carefully at the boy's face before making his decision.

"The boy is right," he said finally, in a very quiet voice. "I promised to fill his can and that is what I will do. Let it not be said that the Duke of Zo broke his promise to anyone, certainly not this very small boy."

He turned to the men gathered at the top of the stairs and called them all into the cellar.

"All of you, come here and help. Fill the can to the very brim. Broach every cask in the castle, if need be, but this can shall be filled."

Dozens of men scrambled into the cellar and one by one they began to open the casks. The soldier continued to pour out the wine into the can whilst the others kept replacing empty casks with full ones.

Cask after cask was opened and cask after cask was emptied. But the can was not full.

The men emptying the casks were talking excitedly to each other, none of them quite believing this amazing thing that was happening in front of their eyes. The soldier's arm was beginning to ache and the Duke, looking on in complete disbelief, was not only wondering where all the wine was going, but how such a small boy could continue to hold a can that must, by now, be very heavy. Yet still, not a drop of wine had fallen on the floor.

At last every cask except one was empty and the can was almost full.

The soldier looked at the Duke and the Duke looked at the boy. This was the cask with the red square on it; this was the finest wine in the land; this was the wine treasured above all others. The Duke thought of asking the boy if he would be satisfied with what he had, for the can was almost full. The boy made no move but still held the can tightly in his hand. The Duke refused to break his word.

"Open it," he commanded, and the last cask was broached.

Slowly, they poured the precious liquid into the tiny can and, as the last drop slipped from the cask, they all saw that the can was full. The Duke sighed and the soldier mopped his brow.

"There's your wine, boy," said the Duke and his tone was still gentle, even though his whole stock of wine had been used up. "Take it to your mother and I hope it will make her well again."

"She will be, sir," replied the boy and, with a hop and a jump, he was up the stairs and through the door, perilously balancing his brimming can of wine.

The Duke looked round at all his men and nobles who had moved quickly out of the way as the tiny, agile boy slipped swiftly through.

"Now to beat the Prince's enemies!" he roared, and led the way out to the courtyard and the waiting horses.

By riding and marching for many days, the Duke's armies arrived at the borders of his cousin's land. They rested there whilst the Duke sent out scouts to bring back news about the rebel army that had conquered most of the Province.

As soon as they were rested, they engaged the enemy and forced them to retreat. Victory after victory they won until the rebels grew frightened at the very sound of the Duke's name. They battled their way across the land, defeating the enemy wherever they stopped to fight and chasing them hard when they did not.

After three months they finally reached the palace and the Duke's cousin was safe. But although the palace had been recaptured and the Prince was safe, the rebel army had not yet been finally defeated.

They had been driven into one corner of the land and the Chief was furious that they had lost so much land in such a short time. He blamed the Duke and offered a large reward to anyone who could capture him.

Because the armies had been so successful, the Duke was able to send for some of the grooms to attend to the horses and for stewards and serving men to attend to the nobles and the soldiers who had fought so hard.

Now, among those stewards who travelled to the Prince's land was that very same, surly steward who had first discovered the boy in the Castle of Zoclan. He had never forgotten how the Duke had spoken to him in front of the others and, what is more, he had never forgiven him.

He heard about the great quantity of gold that was being offered for the capture of the Duke and began to think of ways of collecting the reward and gaining his revenge at the same time. Patiently, he waited for his chance.

It was several weeks before it came and then, one day, some rebels were being sent back to their own land in exchange for soldiers from the army of the Duke. The steward sent a message by one of the rebels telling their chief what he wanted in return for betraying the Duke.

He demanded twice the amount of gold and a high position in the Chief's army and, so anxious were the rebels to be rid of the Duke, the Chief agreed.

Shortly afterwards a fierce battle took place in which the Duke's armies captured another town and, worn out with the ferocity of the battle, the Duke was resting in his newly-won town. He was sleeping very soundly indeed, for the surly steward had drugged his wine and the wine of his guards and now they were all spread out on the floor of a captured castle, quite unconscious and helpless.

The steward made sure that none of the guards had remained awake and then whistled very softly. Two rebel soldiers, dressed in the uniforms of the Duke's army, appeared driving a cart filled with hay. Swiftly they ran inside and, together, lifted the huge body of the Duke and carried him to the cart. They covered him with the hay and all three set off for the rebel land.

They reached a bridge that crossed a wide river without being stopped.

This bridge marked the limit of the

Duke's advance and soldiers of his army were guarding the way across. On the other side the rebels were still assembled in force. Slowly, the cart pulled up to the bridge and there they were stopped by a troop of horsemen. A Sergeant rode up to them.

"What is your business at this time of night?" queried the Sergeant, "and what are you doing with a hay cart?"

The steward felt his heart beating hard inside him but he had prepared himself for such a question and answered craftily.

"I need to talk to you privately, Sergeant," he said. "We are on the Duke's business and we need your help. These two are spies pretending to escape from the Duke's army and I am hoping that the rebels will believe our story when we get to the other side of the bridge. It would help to convince them if you and some of your troopers could chase us part of the way over the bridge."

The Sergeant considered the matter very carefully but he had seen the steward in the Duke's castle and, finally, he agreed. So it was that a troop of the Duke's own horsemen chased the great Duke across the bridge and into the hands of the waiting enemy and, as the steward looked back, a triumphant smile spread across his face.

He was welcomed with great honour by the Chief of the rebels who presented him with his reward. In the meantime the Duke was thrown into prison until the day should come for him to be executed in the public square.

For three long, miserable days, the Duke lay in prison in a strong rebel castle waiting for the fateful day, while his armies searched the land for a trace of their leader.

On the evening of the third day, the steward came to see him and, with a sneer on his face, told him that he would die the next day and his revenge would be complete.

Of course, he had made sure that the Duke was tied too securely for him to run any risk of being dealt with in the manner that he deserved.

He had made sure of that before even thinking of entering the dungeon.

The day of the public execution arrived. Crowds of rebels gathered in the square together with large numbers of the people who had been forced to assemble and watch. In truth, they would rather be cheering the Duke of Zo and prayed for the day when the Prince would rule over them again.

The executioner tied the rope to the pole at the top of the gallows and two rebels led the Duke to his place beneath the rope. The rebels laughed at him and threw stones, for this was the man who had stopped their rebellion and taken back so much of the land they had taken from the Prince.

They forced the people to shout and jeer at this once mighty Duke.

Although he was bound with stout ropes, the rebels took no chances with such an enemy. They held their spears ready at his back in case his mighty strength should burst the bonds that held him.

The Chief arrived and took his place next to the surly steward who was smirking at his former master.

The crowd fell silent. The moment had arrived. The chief gave the signal to the executioner who fitted the rope around the neck of the famous Duke of Zo.

Close to the Chief, the crowd parted suddenly. All heads turned as if they had been switched on.

In front of the gallows stood a little figure in a cloak of brown, with just a smudge of green. Nobody had seen him arrive but there he stood.

The executioner stopped tying the rope and stared at this strange little man, who turned his head and looked directly at the steward, who gazed back with fear and recognition in his eyes. Then the Chief met the little man's eyes and found himself unable to avert his gaze.

Last of all, the little man looked at the Duke, who stared back without flinching.

Suddenly, the little man began to laugh and sing and whistle in turns, waving to the people in the crowd as he did so. Unable to help hemselves, the people started to sing with him and to laugh and to whistle; and even the rebel soldiers joined in. The little man turned back to the Duke and in a high, piping voice that could be heard above all the noise of singing and whistling and laughing, called out to him:

Duke of Zo: Rise and go.

The rope fell away from the condemned man's neck, the bonds dropped from his wrists and he stepped down from the scaffold where he had been about to die.

The little man pointed a long finger at the steward and skipped over to the Duke. Before the astonished gaze of the great crowd who, rebels and people alike, were cheering every move he made, he lifted the giant of a man on to his tiny back and capered off down the road and out of sight.

The Duke has very little idea what happened next except that he is sure he heard somebody cry:

"WHOOPITY STOORIE."

Whether he did or not we will never know but he did find himself sitting beside the wall of his own castle of Zoclan and in exactly the same spot where he had first met, and believed, the story of a ragged boy more than a year before. By his side, in rags, was the steward who had tried to be a nobleman but had only succeeded in being a traitor.

As the Duke realised where he was, he heard—definitely, this time—a soft voice singing in the wind:

One good turn will always deserve another;
Take this for your kindness to my mother.

The Duke rose and entered his castle. Within the next few weeks, his great army returned from his cousin's land, bringing with them many precious gifts, including a great number of casks of fine wine, one of which was marked with a red square.

In the castle they found one former steward busily cleaning every room thoroughly from top to bottom; and there are so many rooms in the castle that by the time he had finished the last, it was time to start on the first again.

One room only he was never made to clean because it never became dirty. This was the cellar where the new wine was kept, cask upon cask upon cask.

These casks are replaced as soon as they become empty and another one is opened ready for the Duke's use when he entertains in his great castle. So far the one with the red square has not been used and nobody is quite sure what it is being saved for.

One thing everybody does know is that right in the middle of the cellar floor, with a clear space left all round, raised on a polished stool, there is a tiny can which, by the orders of the Duke of Zo, must always be kept filled, right to the very brim.

BOGGARTS UNDERGROUND

It was market day in Maverley and Thomas had come to sell his crop of fruit. His friend, Sandy, had helped him pick the fruit and pack it and had even lent him his horse and cart to bring the crop to market.

They had had a very good day. The fruit was all sold, the horse was back in the shafts and all Sandy needed now was Thomas.

But Thomas was nowhere to be found. He was so fond of singing and dancing and generally being very happy that every time he met an old friend they laughed and chatted with each other without ever thinking about the way time was passing. Poor Sandy could not leave the horse, now that he had him all ready for the return journey and he was just beginning to wonder if he would have to unhitch him and put him back in the stable while he went to look for Thomas, when he heard the singing that he knew so well. Thomas was wandering along the street, singing his heart out, while every so often he did a little jig, sometimes nearly falling over in the process.

"It's thirsty work, Sandy," he called out to his friend. "We need a little drink before we set off."

"I think you've had enough," replied Sandy. "What kept you so long?"

"I was following this little voice," said Thomas. "Everywhere I went someone was singing and I'm sure it called my name. Do you not hear it?"

"The only singing I can hear is what you're doing," muttered Sandy, gruffly. "Now come on with you. We've a long way to go and it's getting dark already."

Sandy was right. The late summer sun was sinking fast and it would be pitch black long before they were anywhere near home. He could imagine the people in their village sympathising with him and saying to each other:

"That Thomas will be rhyming and dancing and poor Sandy will be trying to stop him spending all his money in every Inn they come to."

Indeed that was just what Sandy was trying to do, for no sooner had they left the town than Thomas began telling him of the Leatherbottle Inn, only half a mile from the town, where they could quench their thirst and satisfy their hunger; and perhaps join in with some singing and dancing as well.

"It's no more than a few yards, man," cried Thomas, "and we'll have to eat before we get home or we'll faint on the way."

"There's not much chance of that in your case," replied Sandy. "And what will your wife think when you get home without the money for the fruit?"

"What a miserable man you are," laughed Thomas. "I've plenty of money in my pocket and only a tiny part will be spent at the Inn."

By this time they had almost reached the Leatherbottle Inn and Thomas jumped down and strode off, determined to eat and drink before going any further.

"We'll not have time for hanging

about," pleaded Sandy. "We must get home before it's too dark and we have to pass the hill."

Thomas laughed and slapped his friend on the back:

*We'll eat a bit and drink a bit
And maybe sing and dance.*

He stopped quite suddenly as both he and Sandy heard this little, clear voice finish the verse for them:

*Then wait a bit and rest a bit
Now while we have the chance.*

Sandy was the first to recover from the shock and he made for the door of the Leatherbottle Inn as fast as his legs would carry him.

Thomas was not very far behind him although he did keep looking around to see if there was any sign of the singer. He caught his friend by the doorway and laughed at the startled expression on Sandy's face.

"Come on now," he cried. "We'll stay no more than half an hour and it's nearly dark now so we'll not be home while the light lasts anyway."

"I hope you'll remember that not all the money belongs to you," muttered Sandy who was half inclined to go home on his own without waiting for Thomas.

"It was my fruit, wasn't it?" replied Thomas.

"Certainly it was but I helped to pick it and I helped to pack it; and it was my horse and cart that brought it to town. And we agreed that I was to have my share of what we sold it for."

"So you shall. You will have your share and I'll pay for the food and drink out of mine. We'll stay for half an hour and then I'll give you all the money to keep for us until we get home."

This sounded like a good idea to Sandy. If he had all the money in his pocket perhaps he could lead Thomas past all the other Inns on the road. He could always walk on if Thomas stopped and, without any money, he would have to follow. So he agreed and turned to push open the door of the Leatherbottle Inn, which swung open on its own and he scarcely had time to be surprised when the noise of chatter and laughter quite removed it from his mind. Had the noise not been so loud he might have heard a little chuckle followed by a little song:

Now Thomas has lost all track of time
As he eats and drinks his fill.
I'll bring him to talk in his famous rhyme
At our yearly revels in the hill.

Alas, poor Sandy! He knew he had a problem trying to get Thomas past all the Inns but he had no idea that somebody was actually trying to slow them down until it was time to lead them to the hill. If he had known he would not have stopped at all but gone straight home.

It was nearly two hours later that they left the Leatherbottle Inn and started out on the road to their village of Drechin. It was now very dark and as they travelled, houses and barns were being locked up for the night, lights were going on in bedroom windows and people were off to bed. Sandy sighed.

"That's where we should be," he said, pointing to the lights, "where all sensible people should be—in bed."

But Thomas still wanted to stay longer and whenever they found an Inn that was still open he pressed Sandy to stay.

"It will liven us up," he explained. "We'll travel all the faster for a bit of refreshment inside us."

But Sandy now had control. As soon as they had left the Leatherbottle Inn he had made Thomas keep his promise and hand over the rest of the money which he had put safely in his pocket; and there it was going to stay until they arrived home. In spite of all Thomas's appeals, he remained firm; the money stayed in his pocket and Thomas was led swiftly past all the Inns on the road to Drechin.

Soon, they were approaching the village which meant they were nearly home but it also meant they were close to the hill and Sandy began glancing around anxiously as if expecting something unusual to happen or, worse still, something frightening. Even the horse seemed anxious and trudged along on leaden shoes, more and more unwilling to go any further. Thomas was dozing and occasionally snoring. The clock from a distant church sounded midnight and Thomas stirred in his broken sleep. Sandy tried to get the horse to go faster but the animal seemed more unwilling than ever.

Outside the village of Drechin there was a high hill which the villagers visited during the summer—but only by daylight. Nobody went near the hill at this time of night and Sandy began to think about going a very long way round so as to miss passing the hill itself. His mind was made up for him by Thomas suddenly waking up, starting to sing in a loud voice and jumping off the cart. He ran in a stumbling way towards the hill calling to Sandy:

Why didn't I finish the dance, Sandy?
Why didn't I finish the reel?

Because you dragged me from the dance, Sandy,
Because you dragged me from the keel.

Sandy called to him to keep quiet but Thomas was happy and when Thomas was happy, nothing would keep him quiet. At that moment, the horse decided he would go no further and Sandy was forced to jump off and run after Thomas calling to him all the time. Because Sandy had not heard the little voice in the Leather-bottle Inn, it did not occur to him that Thomas was being led further and further along the little rise that led to the hill itself—and he was following him—long past the time that anybody visited the hill!

For the Hill of Drechin, according to the people in the nearby villages, is a special place. It is the place where the small people live and after midnight the land is considered to be theirs. Nobody quite knows how the agreement was reached but all the villagers for miles around know about it and keep to it. If they do not trouble the small people after midnight, the small people do not trouble the villagers at all.

Yet here was Sandy approaching the hill, with midnight already past, and with Thomas, making enough noise to attract everybody's attention and certain to be heard by those whose ears were the sharpest in the land.

Sandy caught up with Thomas who promptly fell to the ground, still muttering his songs to himself as he stretched his full length on the grass. The moon suddenly flicked out from behind a cloud, making strange black shadows on the ground and lighting up bushes to look like crouching animals. Sandy gulped hard and tried to lift Thomas from the ground but instead found himself pulled down to join his friend. He tried to get to his feet, he tried to lift Thomas to his feet, he tried to persuade him to get up, he threatened that he would go on alone. The only response Thomas made—and the one that Sandy least wanted to hear—was to start singing again:

Why didn't I finish the dance, Sandy?
Why didn't I finish the reel?

"Ssh! Ssh!" whispered Sandy desperately, "you'll wake everybody in the place."

"Nobody lives on top of a hill," said Thomas, sleepily. "Who ever heard of anyone living on top of a hill?"

"But this is the Hill of Drechin. Don't you remember?"

"Of course I remember. The village is down below. We'll rest for five minutes and then go home."

Sandy gave it up and argued no more. Carefully, he looked all around before sitting down again. It was only when he felt the smooth, comfortable grass that he realised how tired he was. The long journey, the trouble of getting Thomas past all the Inns and now the worry of being on the Hill of Drechin after midnight had made him as tired as Thomas. He felt too tired ever to get up again. Slowly his eyes closed, his head dropped back on the grass and he went to sleep.

He had no idea how long he slept but when he woke up the grass was cold and damp. As his eyes became accustomed to the light, he turned to where Thomas had been sleeping. There was no-one there. He sat up in horror. He was alone at the top of the Hill of Drechin in the middle of the night. He tried to speak but only a little croaking sound came out. He did not bother to try again for fear that the wrong people might hear and come looking for them.

Slowly and carefully, he rose to his feet and turned towards the village; and then he stood stock still in shivering fright. Not fifteen yards away stood a large, dark bush and beside that bush something had stirred. His legs had changed to sticks of jelly, his heart bumped in his body like a hammer, his eyes strained towards the bush. He was quite unable to move.

Then the dark, black shape moved again and Sandy clenched his teeth to stop them from chattering. The figure turned quickly in his direction and a hand flashed in the spotted light.

"Is that you, Sandy? Will you come and listen to this?"

Sandy almost collapsed with relief

at the sound of Thomas's voice but then he was in a temper because he had been so frightened. He walked unsteadily to where Thomas was standing by the bush.

"You could have wakened me, couldn't you? I might have caught cold lying on that grass; and I nearly died of fright when I woke up."

"Ssh! Will you listen to this?"

Thomas was standing with his ear turned towards the bush, listening with a look of great attention on his face.

"Stand just there and you'll hear it as well," he told Sandy.

Sandy did as he was told and after a few seconds of hearing nothing at all, the faint sounds of music began to creep up to him. Gradually the music became louder and he recognised voices. Then he heard laughter and finally he could hear it all: singing and clapping and music and laughing and all the noise of great merriment rising up to him from below the ground. He listened for several moments, as enchanted as Thomas himself, and then he tugged at his friend's sleeve.

"Where does it come from?" he asked.

Thomas pointed into the centre of the bush and there Sandy saw a black hole about the size of a wastepaper basket. As he watched, the hole became brighter and he fancied he could see lights and tiny, glistening, shiny sparks. He tugged again at Thomas's sleeve.

"Come on," he said, "or they will see us here and then we shall be in trouble."

But Thomas did not want to leave. At the very least, he wanted to have a closer look. Whilst Sandy held him round the waist, he pushed his head further and further into the hole until Sandy could only see his shoulders.

"Come back!" he whispered. "Come back."

"I can't," came a muffled voice. "You'll have to pull me."

"I am pulling as hard as I can; but something is pulling from the other side."

It was indeed. Sandy held on until the last moment as his friend's shoulders, then his back and then his legs disappeared through the hole in the bush. He looked about him wildly, fearing that his arm would be pulled next. But the pressure stopped as soon as Thomas disappeared.

He was really alone now. Down below, the village was dark. Not a light shone in any house. For a moment he thought of following Thomas but when he looked it was too late: the hole had gone, the bush had closed, the music had stopped.

He turned and rushed headlong down the hill.

His first thought was to rouse the village and take them to the hilltop to rescue Thomas; to search all through that bush and find the hole where he had been sucked in by something much stronger than either of them.

But when he came to his own house he stopped. He was not too keen on going back to the hillside. The people would never believe him, especially if he spoilt their night's sleep. Anyway, the hole had gone. He remembered looking before he left and the hole had definitely gone. There was nothing they could do until it was daylight and it was all Thomas's fault for keeping them out so late.

He suddenly felt very tired and the thought of his bed so close was very tempting. He went indoors and in five minutes was fast asleep.

The next morning when he came downstairs he found a crowd of villagers had gathered outside his house. They stared at him and when he spoke to them, they shrugged their shoulders and started to walk away. One person did not walk away.

"There he is, Sergeant," cried Thomas's wife, "arrest him."

"Now, don't let us be too quick," came the deep tones of the Sergeant. "What am I to arrest him for?"

"For doing away with my Thomas, that's why."

Sandy was shocked that anybody could think he would harm his friend.

He was the one who had tried to protect him all through the journey.

It was Thomas who had taken so long and it was Sandy who had urged him to come home.

"I won't stand for that," he cried. "Why should I want to hurt Thomas?

He was my friend."

The crowd had come back by now and had begun to mutter and grumble.

He could see they were not on his side and before he could tell them what had happened, Thomas's wife marched up to him.

"You want reasons, do you? Who went with Thomas to Maverley? You did. Who was with him on the way home? You were. Who was the last one to see him? You were. Who has come home on his own? You have. And Thomas hasn't."

"But I can tell you what happened," pleaded Sandy.

"I daresay you've got a good story."

"Give him a chance," said the Sergeant, "let's hear what he has to say."

As the crowd listened in silence, he told them about the journey home from Maverley, of the night on the hill, how they had heard the music, how Thomas had been pulled through the hole in the bush and how the hole had disappeared when he looked again.

"That's a very convenient hole," sniffed Thomas's wife. "It's there when you want it and gone when you don't."

"It's the truth, I tell you," cried Sandy. "We all know the stories about the hill."

"But you're the only one who reckons he has seen anything."

"That's because nobody else has been up there at that time."

"And I suppose Thomas had all the money you got from the fruit. And I suppose that's all disappeared as well."

Sandy hesitated for a moment and then took the money from his pocket and held it up.

"There is the money. After the Leatherbottle Inn he gave it to me to look after and it's a good job he did or he would have spent it all."

"What more do you want?" demanded Thomas's wife. "Thomas is missing and he has all the money."

The Sergeant was not sure because if Sandy had meant to steal the money why would he show it now? Why would he come back to his own house? On the other hand, although the villagers knew the stories about the hill, nobody would really admit they believed them. But then, as Sandy said, nobody went up there at midnight.

"If you don't believe me," said Sandy, softly, "why not come with me tonight, at midnight, to the hill and listen?"

It was suddenly very quiet, with everybody looking at each other, uneasily. Nobody wanted to go to the hill at midnight but nobody wanted to admit it.

"Well," said Thomas's wife, grudgingly, "I suppose we could go there now and search for any signs."

"Yes, yes; that's a good idea," said several of the crowd and some suggested splitting up into smaller groups. Others did not like that and thought they should all stay together.

In the end, they searched every day for a week but found no sign of Thomas. They did find Sandy's horse but he was half a mile away from where Sandy had left him. Sandy himself stood by the bush for hours, but he could not find the hole and he could not hear music. At last they called off the search and Thomas's wife had the money.

Sandy knew that most of the people in the village thought it was his fault. Many of them thought that something strange had happened that night but they could not quite believe his story. Nearly everybody ignored him; when he went to the shop, Mrs. Carter served him but said as little as possible; some even thought he was bewitched and held their children's hands tightly when he approached. He thought of moving house and visited the other villages to see if there were houses for sale.

Exactly a year passed by and he was preparing to go and look at another house when he saw two men setting out on the road to Maverley with their cart piled high with fruit to be sold at market. He remembered with a start that Thomas was still lost and that it was at this time, a year ago, when he and Thomas had set out for town.

The idea came into his head that this was the best time to search when things were the same as they had been a year ago.

He decided to go back and talk

about his idea to Thomas's wife but before he could move he noticed a tiny movement at the side of the road and thought he saw a faint smudge of brown and green that seemed to be dancing.

What he certainly heard was the same little voice that had finished Thomas's rhyme, a year ago, outside the Leatherbottle Inn.

"Sandy, Sandy" came the small voice:

Join us tonight for our revels are bound
And away from the hill shall we roam,
Save for the master who sleeps in the mound,
And ... Thomas, who waits to come home.

Sandy was frightened; but he was also excited. He knew that his idea was a good one. He knew that he must go back to the hill, even if he went on his own. But if nobody else came with him, he would have the same trouble as last year: nobody would believe him.

He tried hard to persuade Thomas's wife but, although she wanted to go and see where her husband had disappeared, she could not pluck up enough courage to go there at midnight.

He asked other people in the village, but they all shook their heads.

At last, he asked the Sergeant and he agreed, but said it would be much better if others could see for themselves.

When the two of them were ready to set out, just a little before midnight, first one and then two, and then more, fell in beside them until twenty or thirty curious—but uneasy

—villagers made their way to the Hill of Drechin.

The moon was flitting between the clouds as they reached the area of the bush and settled themselves to wait.

Shadows danced across the ground and small trees bent and groaned in the rising wind.

Bushes and ragged stones made strange, gaunt shapes against the dark green grass. Every sound of the leaves or the movement of some tiny animal sounded like the approach of an army of giants.

The lights in the village below went out one by one until, at last, they were the only human beings awake that night, high, near the top of Drechin Hill.

The Sergeant shuffled painfully on the damp, cold grass; the moon went in behind a deep black cloud and, in the distance, the church clock struck twelve o'clock.

Sandy lifted his finger and listened. Far away it seemed, but rising steadily to his ears, came the sound of music, then laughter, then clapping and great merriment. First it came to Sandy's ears and then to everybody else, standing like statues in rapt amazement.

"Ssh!" whispered Sandy and led the way to the bush. There, in the centre of the bush, just as he had described it, was the hole the size of a wastepaper basket and from this hole, rising through the ground came the sounds of revelry and enjoyment.

They all crowded round and presently they could see little shapes, dancing and singing, all holding hands. In the walls where Sandy had seen the glistening sparks, he now saw burning candles.

Then, as if by some command, the people began to move back from the hole; back and away from the bush.

They crept across the hill and knelt behind other clumps of bushes. For the little people were coming nearer and nearer the hole. Every circle of their dance was bringing them nearer and nearer the entrance. Every tune and every song brought them closer to the watchers in the bushes.

Then, as the bright moonlight flashed out from the deep black cloud, they burst into the gaze of the watching villagers.

Dancing in joy they came, all hands together, all keeping the time, every circle perfect in its shape.

Keeping time, in the middle of the throng, dancing and singing as happily as the rest, came...Thomas! Thomas the Rhymer, his big, bass voice blending with the high pipings of his little friends!

Sandy crept from the bushes and slipped cautiously along the ground.

From tree to tree he went until he

stood within arm's reach of Thomas himself. Slowly he stretched out his hand, inch by inch, until it rested on the collar of the Rhymer's coat. Then he jerked with all his might, held his friend in a grip of steel and hung on for all he was worth.

In a flash, the music stopped; the Boggarts vanished. The villagers, slowly overcoming their fear, tip-toed towards the tree where Sandy held his captive tight.

Great was their rejoicing when they saw that Thomas was safe and sound.

To Sandy they all apologised for doubting him although his story had seemed very strange. As for Thomas, he could not understand why they had come so soon to stop him enjoying his revels:

Couldn't I finish the dance, Sandy?
Couldn't I finish the reel?

And a tiny voice joined with him:

*Because you dragged him from the
dance, Sandy;
Because you dragged him from the
keel.*

To this day, Thomas will not believe he was away for a whole year.

To him, as to the Boggarts, it was just one night; a night of singing and dancing with the little people in their Inn below the ground.